LUMPY POI AND
TWISTING EELS

BOOK 2 IN THE
KANAʻIAUPUNI SERIES

Lumpy Poi and Twisting Eels

The Story of Kamehameha's Early Childhood

THE STORY OF KAMEHAMEHA'S EARLY CHILDHOOD

DAVID KĀWIKA EYRE

ILLUSTRATED BY
IMAIKALANI KALAHELE

KAMEHAMEHA PUBLISHING

HONOLULU

The Kanaʻiaupuni Series is a work of historical fiction about Kamehameha, the great hero of Hawaiʻi. The series highlights the people, places, and events that shaped Kamehameha's life and led him to become the Conqueror of the Islands. The stories are based on Hawaiian sources and are intended for students, families, and educators.

KAMEHAMEHA SCHOOLS

Inquiries should be addressed to:
Kamehameha Publishing
567 S. King Street
Honolulu, Hawaiʻi 96813

ISBN 978-0-87336-154-5

Design by Viki Nasu Design Group

Printed in China

12 11 10 09 08 07   1 2 3 4 5

To my colleagues at Kamehameha Schools
May we teach as Naeʻole taught

THE STORY TO THIS POINT...

Before Kamehameha's birth, his mother Keku'iapoiwa craves the eye of the man-eating niuhi shark. Alapa'inui, the great chief of Hawai'i, learns of this craving and knows it is a sign. If the child is allowed to live, he will become a slayer of chiefs and a conqueror of islands. Under pressure from lesser chiefs, Alapa'inui orders his executioners to kill the boy at his first breath.

But Keku'iapoiwa will never let this happen. In secret, she summons her attendant Nae'ole, a young and trusted chief of Kohala. They wrap the newborn in kapa, and Nae'ole slips away with the bundle into the darkness of early morning. The child is hidden in a cave in the hills at 'Āwini, where a woman named Kaha cares for him. Kaha and Nae'ole risk their lives to shelter the royal Kamehameha.

In this story, Kaha and Nae'ole secretly move to Hālawa where Kamehameha spends his first years of childhood.

t was a time when the land of Hālawa on the Island of Hawai'i hid the high-ranking child Kamehameha, the boy who would one day become Kana'iaupuni, the Conqueror of the Islands.

At Kamehameha's birth, ruling chief Alapa'inui had sent executioners with orders to kill, for it was prophesied that if this baby lived, he would grow up to become a great niuhi shark of the land, a killer of chiefs and a ruler of islands.

Hālawa was the land of Kamehameha's mother Keku'iapoiwa—the mother he did not know. In the first moments of his life, she had sent Kamehameha away to save him from Alapa'inui's guards and their killing hands.

The people of Hālawa held this secret in their eyes. Their families had long been of this land. They were kama'āina. From the corners of their eyes they watched. If an intruder came, they would know.

A well-worn path led to Hālawa. On the hillside above, among the trees, a lookout kept guard, a conch shell at hand. If a stranger approached, the lookout blew into the pū, sending a sound like a warning wind to the people below.

At day's end, when all was well, a call came from the hill: "Makani! Makani!" The people of Hālawa knew their beloved Kamehameha was safe.

This land was wet and fat and fed its people well.

Hālawa was a lush, watered land. Taro waved and glittered in terraced loʻi set along the stream. Red and green sugarcane stood in clumps, and banana stalks leaned from the weight of bunches. Near the ridges there were breadfruit trees, their bulging fruits hanging heavy among big leaves. In the clearings upslope from the water, sweet potatoes mounded the stony soil.

The stream ran among smooth gray rocks, down a pebbled beach, and into the sea. To each side, cliffs dropped into deep blue water where silver ulua glinted. This land was wet and fat and fed its people well. Their eyes were never half closed from hunger.

Kamehameha lived here with his ʻohana. The houses of his kauhale, shaded by large kamani trees, stood inland, well above the rocks where the black crabs live.

Kamehameha was one of many splashing, scampering keiki whose play was heard through the trees. "'O ʻoe ke akua! 'O ʻoe ke akua! You're it! You're it!" they yelled in voices that sometimes brought stern "Kulikuli!" scoldings from their elders. The chosen "akua" pressed her eyes into her arm and patted the coconut trunk in a steady drumming beat, allowing the other children to rush off and hide as she called out:

"Kuʻi, kuʻi, hana pele!
Holo i uka, holo i kai!
Holo i kahi e peʻe ai,
A nalo!"

"Pound, pound, make it smooth!
Run to the hills, run to the sea!
Run to a hiding place I can't see,
And vanish!"

Kamehameha played hard, smiled wide, and spent much of the day rushing about out of breath. This aliʻi boy ran as well as he swam, but the quickest boy of all was Makoa, he who would one day become Kamehameha's trusted runner.

By day's end, prints of small feet marked the darkening land of Hālawa. At night, the sleep song Kaha sang when Kamehameha was a baby could still be heard from his hale: "The birds are going to sleep … The flowers are going to sleep … The fish are ready to sleep …"

In those early years, the people of Hālawa knew Kamehameha as a high-ranking aliʻi, a boy of noble genealogy and great mana. Though he was strong of body and keenly intelligent, the keiki treated him the same as other children. Hidden among his people, he was expected to be one of them. In spite of his rank, he played the games of the children, he worked alongside his people, and they respected him for it.

Much of what Kamehameha learned in Hālawa would make him the chief he later became.

In time, Kamehameha passed from the care of women and the play of children to the company of men. He rode the shoulders of his kahu, Naeʻole, a chief of Hālawa who had cared for him since birth. Naeʻole's arms gleamed brown like hard, polished

wood and easily swung the boy up on his broad shoulders. Kamehameha came to know the world from there and to understand that much was expected of him.

When Kamehameha was old enough to carry two coconuts, he began to learn the chants of daily life and the rich stories of his people, his ʻaumākua, his akua. He learned of the sea and the land, of fishing and planting. Naeʻole was his teacher. When Naeʻole spoke, Kamehameha would watch, listen, then do, and say very little.

Naeʻole taught Kamehameha to paddle a canoe and to fish for aku. "These are the days of rain," Naeʻole explained. "The lehua flowers bloom in the sea." He spoke few words and did not call the fish by name. "The fish have ears," he would say. Speaking of fishing would bring bad luck. Instead of aku, he spoke of lehua flowers blooming in the sea.

They paddled to where terns circled and screeched. The aku
were there, driving small fish to the surface. They let out hand
lines, out and out, skimming a pearl-shell lure through the water.
The first aku took the hook in its hard mouth. Kamehameha,
with the arms of a small boy, needed help from Nae'ole to pull
the bulky, jerking fish into the canoe. Nae'ole held the shiny aku
down, clubbed it dead, cut off its tail, and laid it in the bow of
the canoe.

"This is the first fish," he said. "It is kapu. When we return to
shore we will go to the shrine. We will offer the fish to Kū'ula
and our 'aumākua."

The sea shivered with fish. As the canoe kept with the aku, the
hook was returned again and again, and the canoe came back
heavy with fish. Nae'ole knew when they had taken enough.
There would always be aku for another day.

Nae'ole taught Kamehameha the season for planting coconuts.
"The sugarcane is tasseling," he said. "The squid are now plenti-
ful. This is the time to plant coconuts."

In the morning light, while the sunshine was still crisp, the man
and the boy bent side by side in work, digging two holes in the
dark dirt. When their bodies glistened with sweat, they ran into
the water, splashing through the cold, oncoming waves. They
returned with two he'e from a fisherman whose basket was full.
Nae'ole spoke: "Place a squid in each hole and spread out its
eight 'awe'awe."

They paddled to where terns circled and screeched.

Kamehameha worked in silence. While he planted, he heard the far-off sounds of the younger children at play: "Pound, pound, make it smooth!" they cried. His own heart pounded with excitement. He wanted to play, not to plant! He looked up and saw his friend Makoa sprinting down the beach. Why, he grumbled, must I be sweating over these small sprouting things?

His kahu interrupted his grumbling: "Set the sprouted nuts next to the he'e in the hole. The he'e will give the roots a firm grip. The coconuts on these trees will grow round and fat like the head of the he'e. They will be the food of your children and your people."

Not long after, Nae'ole taught Kamehameha to grow kalo and make poi. He took the boy to the muddy lo'i by the stream. "See the man. His work is hana kua wehi, black back work, for he labors long in the sun. His back is burned black like mud. It is by the work of our people that the land feeds us. We all must work. Even we who are ali'i. We are ali'i because of the aloha of our people."

Nae'ole stooped and washed his hard hands in the water that fed the lo'i. "Kamehameha, the water is cold. It will soon flow clear through the lo'i. It comes from high in the 'ōhi'a forests. Listen. It chants." They were quiet. Listening.

Nae'ole raised his eyebrows toward the horizon: "The moon is Hua. We will plant tomorrow."

"We all must work. Even we who are aliʻi.
We are aliʻi because of the aloha of our people."

That night Kamehameha snuggled down in his kapa, a kapa white as moonlight. Kaha told the stories Kamehameha loved. The glow of the ihoiho kukui shone on the boy, and his lids grew heavy.

Another woman stepped into the hale. She stood in the shade of the lamplight, looking with love at the boy. Kamehameha gazed at the woman. Their eyes touched for a moment, but sleep lay like a mist over his eyes. Hovering between sleeping and waking as he was, the woman was neither mist nor shade. She sang with Kaha, their voices weaving, blending, softer and softer: "The birds are going to sleep … The flowers are going to sleep … The fish are ready to sleep …" Kamehameha listened … listened till his lashes lay down on his cheeks.

From the pali came the evening call of the lookout: "Makani! Makani!" All was well.

In the morning the men broiled fish, and all ate heartily. When they got to the lo'i, they chanted and planted huli stalks in mounds. The kahu and the boy stood side by side, backs bent. Kamehameha's hands followed Nae'ole's hands.

They worked long. Finally, Nae'ole spoke: "Enough. Go to the next lo'i where the leaves of the kalo have slackened and yellowed. The kalo sits like a squat gourd. Pull it."

Kamehameha did as he was told. He cleaned the kalo in the cold stream. He heard the chant in the water.

That afternoon, he learned to light the imu and heat the stones until they were white hot. After the kalo had cooked in the imu, Kamehameha used a large ʻopihi shell to scrape off the skins while the kalo was still warm.

As he worked, his kahu watched. In the shade of a hau tree, Naeʻole rolled out a mat. He placed the pounding board on it. Next to the board, on ti leaves, he put the pounding stone and a kou bowl filled with water. Without a word, he took a chunk of gray-blue kalo, sat with his legs to each side of the board, and began to mash the kalo with the heavy pounder, rolling the roundness of the stone over the kalo as he pounded.

Kamehameha watched as Naeʻole splashed water, wetting the rounded stone with his hand and pounding the kalo to smoothness. "E nānā mai," Naeʻole said. "The stone goes, the hand follows."

The stone was heavy for Kamehameha. But he managed to mash the kalo, rolling, lifting, dropping the stone, and rolling it again. His hands strained from the weight of the stone. When he thought he was done, he said: "Pau kēia hana iaʻu. I have finished this work."

Naeʻole placed a small kamani bowl of salt on the mat. In the bowl the salt glittered. "Now eat your poi."

With two fingers twisting into the poi, Kamehameha ate. The poi caught in his throat. He laid his hand on his knee and looked down. After a moment he said, "Puʻupuʻu. Lumpy."

"E hele mai. We will follow the stream into the land
and up to the high 'ōhi'a forests."

Nae'ole glanced once at the board: "Eat all of it. Next time you work until there are no lumps left." This Kamehameha did.

And so Kamehameha, the boy who would one day become the great niuhi shark of the battlefield, sat on the mat and ate … ate until there was no more lumpy poi left.

Afterward, Kamehameha and Nae'ole went to the stream. They washed their hands in the cold water, the water that comes out of the land like breath and murmurs in the pebbles.

Nae'ole spoke: "E hele mai. We will follow the stream into the land and up to the high 'ōhi'a forests." They left, Kamehameha's small hand safe in Nae'ole's.

They made their way upland. The stream fell from pool to pebbled pool. They looked up at the falling water, waded the stream, and entered a grove of trees.

"There are two kinds of 'ōhi'a," Nae'ole explained. "They are family, but they are treated differently." Motioning with his head to the trees, Nae'ole continued. "These are 'ōhi'a leo. In this part of the forest we may speak. Go, e ku'u keiki, and pick the mountain apples."

Kamehameha climbed into a tree and tossed down the crimson fruits to his kahu's cupped hands.

They sat on a rock and ate the crisp fruit. "When your mother was young she lived in Hālawa. She was beautiful. We spoke of her as a mountain apple ripened in the shade."

"The day will come, Kamehameha,
when you will wear a cape of mamo feathers."

Kamehameha stared at the silent sunlight and wondered about his mother. He wiped his mouth with the back of his hand.

"We will go higher," Nae'ole said. "When we come to the 'ōhi'a hāmau, we must be silent. I will show you the birds that come for the lehua nectar: the red 'i'iwi and the black mamo. The black mamo has only a few precious yellow feathers. They are kapu to the high chief. The day will come, Kamehameha, when you will wear a cape of mamo feathers. For now, you may not speak a word."

They reached the gray, ancient trees. Trees of crooked branches. Nae'ole looked up to the red bursts of lehua blossoms on the top-most twigs. The birds were flitting there, flickering there. The two ali'i watched without words. Their silence lasted until they got back to shore. They parted near a hale not far from the beach.

The tide was low, the boy was tired. His chin on his hands, he lay alone on the shore looking at a dark rock. A black crab crawled carefully across the rock, its shadow following, its eyes sharp and

suspicious. They watched each other until the boy got up to go. He walked home, passing cautiously around the hale of an old woman who had once scolded him.

The land was dark, the moon was dark. Kamehameha grew drowsy before all the stories were told. As he drifted to sleep, he thought about the lehua blooming in the sea, about planting he'e with the coconuts and pounding poi. He wondered about the black crab. He wondered about the cape made of mamo feathers. And he thought about his mother.

The next day Nae'ole taught Kamehameha to fish for puhi. He showed the boy how to mash, mix and firm the bait and to make the basket trap ready for the night. "The bait must be well made and neat to attract the eel. We will leave the trap in the haunt of the eels."

Early the next morning Nae'ole and Kamehameha went to the beach. The land was light, the moon was light. The trap was filled with twisting eels. They took the trap ashore, poured out the puhi, and struck them with sticks. One blow to the head, another to the tail, and an eel was dead. They lit the imu and let the stones heat white as they gathered ti leaves to wrap the eels. While the puhi cooked, Nae'ole and Kamehameha made poi together for the days to come. Smooth poi with no lumps.

When the eels were baked, men, women and children gathered for prayer. Then, in their separate places, they ate the delicacy until they were full and satisfied. There was much smacking of the lips, for they were very fond of eel.

And so it was that in his kulāiwi, the land of his ancestors, Kamehameha grew and thrived in his first years.

In his kulāiwi, the land of his ancestors,
Kamehameha grew and thrived.

But, when Kamehameha was of an age to carry another child on his back, Nae'ole said he had to leave Hālawa.

"You must go to the court of Alapa'inui in Hilo. He is older now and has changed his mind. He no longer wants your death."

Kamehameha rested his hand on Nae'ole's arm and searched his kahu's face. "But why? Why must I go? This is where I want to be."

Nae'ole could not look down. He gazed instead beyond the boy to where a cloud lay smooth over the mountains. "You must go where the kōlea calls," he said. "You must know your relatives. They are your bone and blood. Alapa'inui will help you to fulfill your destiny. But go first to Kaha. She is your hānai mother. By her words you will understand." This Kamehameha did.

A double canoe was made ready for their journey to Hilo. Kamehameha embraced his people. Sitting next to Kaha was the old woman who had once scolded him. She held out a gourd of water. He drank and felt the cold of the stream in his teeth.

His friend Makoa ran up and handed Kamehameha a beautiful white shell he had saved. The two looked at each other with quiet in their eyes. And they smiled.

"You must go where the kōlea calls," he said.
"You must know your relatives. They are your bone and blood."

The canoe sailed quietly along the dark cliffs of Hāmākua.

Kamehameha stepped onto the canoe and stood beside his kahu. He faced the land and stared at the stream. He dropped his eyes and waited. The afternoon light glared off the lifting paddles.

He did not hear the paddles dip away at the water. He did not hear the wash of waves rushing back to shore. It was the chant of the women that filled his ears as the wind filled the sails.

Later that evening, Nae'ole spoke: "When the night dawns, we will reach the darkly washed sands of Hilo and you will know your mother, Keku'iapoiwa. You will know Keōuakupua, your father, and you will enter the court of Alapa'inui. I must return to Hālawa."

Nae'ole looked long at the boy he loved.

The canoe sailed quietly along the dark cliffs of Hāmākua. But Kamehameha's thoughts had not left the land of the warm food and the full calabash, the place where the cold stream chants.

He looked at his kahu with silent, wondering eyes.

Nae'ole finally answered those eyes with a whisper: "It must be. As the deep sea follows the shallow water, it must be."

Kamehameha's fists clutched the sail cord, those hands that would one day break men's bones. His knuckles went white. He gazed up to where the stars are, and his teeth bit back the tears.

MAHALO

I am indebted to the many kumu—sources or teachers—whose work is the lasting kahua or foundation for all we do. Mary Kawena Pukui is an important if sometimes veiled cultural source for this story, including the game chant, the lullaby, and the 'ōlelo no'eau, or wise sayings, that weave throughout. Samuel M. Kamakau provided facts on taro growing, poi pounding, and eel fishing. I have borrowed from these authors, and others listed in the bibliography, with the greatest respect and gratitude.

Kēhau Cachola-Abad and Matthew Corry have been wonderful in guiding this work to publication. Gavan Daws has been extraordinarily supportive of this project and has my sincere gratitude and aloha for his many contributions. Imaikalani Kalahele has produced images of extraordinary power, cultural complexity, and beauty. Ke'ala Kwan's instinctive cultural insight has helped to focus these stories. Clemi McLaren has been encouraging and generous in every way. Sigrid Southworth has provided constructive criticism and a keen sense of this land. Anna Sumida has contributed enthusiasm and an experienced eye for the needs of young readers.

Others who have supported this project include Sally and Chris Aall, William Ailā, Kiele Akana-Gooch, Julian Ako, Elizabeth Boynton, Fred Cachola, Māhealani Chang, Mike Chun, Megan Clark, Jan Dill, Conard Eyre, David W. Eyre, Gail Fujimoto, Dani Gardner, Melehina Groves, Kaiponohea Hale, Paul Harper, Liana Honda, Lois Long, Kawika Makanani, Tyna Millacci, Terina Morris, Saul Nakayama, Bonnie Ozaki-James, William Kalikolehua Pānui, Mike Racoma, Tad Sewell, Kim and Jim Slagel, Kalani Soller, Oz Stender, Blaine Tolentino, Keola and Ipo Wong, Mimi Wong, and my children: Sintra, Lisa, Emma, Makana, and Alea.

Many students at Kamehameha Schools have provided invaluable assistance with this series. For this book, I especially want to thank Sanoe Keli'inoi, Kaipo Lucas, Kealohapuakanani Mahikō, Le'a Murakami, and Ka'awaloa Sam.

I am grateful to Nā Kumu o Kamehameha, Ka'iwakīloumoku, Ho'okahua, and Kamehameha Publishing for their inspiration and support.

The mistakes that remain are mine alone. Mahalo nui iā 'oukou pākahi a pau.

D. K. E.
September 2007

GLOSSARY

GODS & PEOPLE

Alapaʻinui · ruling chief of Hawaiʻi Island at Kamehameha's birth
Kaha · hānai or foster mother of Kamehameha at his birth
Kamehameha · first chief who would come to unite and rule over the Hawaiian Islands
Kanaʻiaupuni · the Conqueror of the Islands
Kekuʻiapoiwa · mother of Kamehameha
Keōuakupua · father of Kamehameha
Kūʻula · a god of fishing
Makoa · aliʻi from Kohala; Kamehameha's fastest runner
Naeʻole · chief of Kohala who saved Kamehameha's life after his birth

PLACES

ʻĀwini · land section in North Kohala
Hālawa · land section in North Kohala where Kamehameha spent his early childhood
Hāmākua · district, northeast Hawaiʻi Island
Hawaiʻi · largest of the Hawaiian Islands
Hilo · district and bay on eastern Hawaiʻi Island
Kohala · district in northwest Hawaiʻi Island

OTHER HAWAIIAN WORDS

aliʻi · chief, ruler
aloha · love, affection, greeting, good-bye
aku · bonito, skipjack; an important food fish
akua · god
ʻaumakua · (pl. ʻaumākua) ancestral spirit
ʻaweʻawe · tentacles
E hele mai · Come here
E kuʻu keiki · O my beloved child
E nānā mai · Look here
hale · house
hāmau · quiet
hana kua wehi · black back work; hard work
hānai · to adopt, to feed, to nourish
hau · lowland tree of the hibiscus family
heʻe · squid, octopus
Hua · name of the thirteenth night of the lunar moon
huli · taro top, as used for planting

ihoiho kukui · kukui nut candle

'i'iwi · red native Hawaiian bird; a type of honey creeper

imu · underground oven

kahu · guardian

kalo · taro

kama'āina · a person native to a particular place; native-born

kamani · a shade tree whose wood was used for food bowls

kapa · tapa, a cloth made from inner bark

kapu · sacred, restricted, protected

kauhale · a group of houses that together make a Hawaiian home

keiki · child, children

kōlea · Pacific golden plover (a bird)

kou · a shade tree with orange flowers; wood used for food bowls

kulāiwi · homeland, native land

Kulikuli · Be quiet

lehua · the flower of the 'ōhi'a lehua tree

leo · voice, sound

lo'i · irrigated taro pond

makani · wind; call of sentinel, similar to "all's well"

mamo · a native Hawaiian bird, now extinct

mana · supernatural or divine power; spiritual or personal force

niuhi · large, man-eating shark

'O 'oe ke akua · You are "it"

'ohana · extended family

'ōhi'a · common tree producing wood and flowers; also referred to as 'ōhi'a lehua

'opihi · limpet

pali · cliff

Pau kēia hana ia'u · I have finished this work; I am finished with this work

poi · food staple from pounded taro corms

pū · conch or helmet shell

pu'upu'u · lumpy, as in poi

puhi · eel

ulua · crevalle, jackfish; also refers to a man

Ku'i, ku'i, hana pele!	Pound, pound, make it smooth!
Holo i uka, holo i kai!	Run to the hills, run to the sea!
Holo i kahi e pe'e ai,	Run to a hiding place I can't see,
A nalo!	And vanish!

The Hawaiian words in this text have been recorded to make correct pronunciation available to readers and students. Warmest mahalo to Hawaiian language teachers Māhealani Chang and Ke'ala Kwan for recording these words. To hear the glossary, go to http://publishing.ksbe.edu/ and click on the book title link.

SELECTED BIBLIOGRAPHY

The sources listed below form the kahua or foundation of *Lumpy Poi and Twisting Eels*. Though not an exhaustive list, the selected bibliography indicates the key sources consulted for this story and provides a starting point for further research on the life of Kamehameha.

Beckwith, Martha Warren. *Kepelino's Traditions of Hawai'i*. Bernice P. Bishop Museum Bulletin 95. Honolulu: Bishop Museum Press, 1932.

Buck, Peter H. [Te Rangi Hiroa]. *Arts and Crafts of Hawai'i*. Honolulu: Bishop Museum Press, 1957.

Daws, Gavan. *Shoal of Time: A History of the Hawaiian Islands*. Toronto: MacMillan, 1968.

Desha, Stephen Langhern. *Kamehameha and His Warrior Kekūhaupi'o*. Translated by Frances N. Frazier. Honolulu: Kamehameha Schools Press, 2000.

Elbert, Samuel H., Esther T. Mookini, and Mary Kawena Pukui. *Place Names of Hawai'i*. 2nd ed. Honolulu: University of Hawai'i Press, 1974.

Handy, Edward Smith Craighill, and Elizabeth Green Handy. With Mary Kawena Pukui. *Native Planters in Old Hawai'i: Their Life, Lore, and Environment*. Bernice P. Bishop Museum Bulletin 233. Honolulu: Bishop Museum Press, 1972.

Handy, Edward Smith Craighill, and Mary Kawena Pukui. *The Polynesian Family System in Ka'ū, Hawai'i*. Rutland, VT: Charles E. Tuttle, 1972.

Ii, John Papa. *Fragments of Hawaiian History*. Edited by Dorothy Benton Barrère. Translated by Mary Kawena Pukui. Honolulu: Bishop Museum Press, 1959.

Judd, Walter F. *Kamehameha*. Edited by Robert B. Goodman and Robert A. Spicer. Hong Kong: Mandarin Ltd., 1976.

Kalākaua, David. *Legends and Myths of Hawai'i*. Rutland, VT: Charles E. Tuttle, 1972.

Kamakau, Samuel Mānaiakalani. *Ruling Chiefs of Hawai'i*. Honolulu: Kamehameha Schools Press, 1961.

Kamakau, Samuel Mānaiakalani. *Ka Poʻe Kahiko: The People of Old.* Edited by Dorothy Benton Barrère. Translated by Mary Kawena Pukui. Honolulu: Bishop Museum Press, 1964.

———. *Tales and Traditions of the People of Old: Nā Moʻolelo a ka Poʻe Kahiko.* Honolulu: Bishop Museum Press, 1991.

———. *The Works of the People of Old: Nā Hana a ka Poʻe Kahiko.* Honolulu: Bishop Museum Press, 1976.

Kanahele, George Heʻeu Sanford. *Kū Kanaka, Stand Tall: A Search for Hawaiian Values.* Honolulu: University of Hawaiʻi Press, 1986.

Kāne, Herb Kawainui. *Ancient Hawaiʻi.* Captain Cook, HI: Kawainui Press, 1997.

———. *Voyagers.* Edited by Paul Berry. Bellevue, WA: WhaleSong, 1991.

Kōmike Huaʻōlelo, Hale Kuamoʻo, ʻAha Pūnana Leo. *Māmaka Kaiao: A Modern Hawaiian Vocabulary.* Honolulu: University of Hawaiʻi Press, 1998.

Kuykendall, Ralph S. *The Hawaiian Kingdom.* Vol. 1, *1778–1854, Foundation and Transformation.* Honolulu: University of Hawaiʻi Press, 1938.

Malo, David. *Hawaiian Antiquities.* 2nd ed. Translated by Nathaniel B. Emerson. Bernice P. Bishop Museum Special Publication 2. Honolulu: Bishop Museum Press, 1951.

McKinzie, Edith Kawelo Kapule. "An Original Narrative of Kamehameha the Great, Written in *Ka Naʻi Aupuni* (1905–1906) by Joseph M. Poepoe." Master's thesis, University of Hawaiʻi–Mānoa, 1982.

Mellen, Kathleen Dickenson. *The Lonely Warrior.* New York: Hastings House, 1949.

Pukui, Mary Kawena. *ʻŌlelo Noʻeau: Hawaiian Proverbs and Poetical Sayings.* Bernice P. Bishop Museum Special Publication 71. Honolulu: Bishop Museum Press, 1983.

Pukui, Mary Kawena, and Samuel H. Elbert. *Hawaiian Dictionary.* 2nd ed. Honolulu: University of Hawaiʻi Press, 1986.

Pukui, Mary Kawena, E. W. Haertig, and Catherine A. Lee. *Nānā i Ke Kumu: Look to the Source.* 2 vols. Honolulu: Queen Liliʻuokalani Children's Center–Hui Hānai, 1979.

Tregaskis, Richard. *The Warrior King.* New York: MacMillan, 1973.

KAMEHAMEHA
PUBLISHING

AMPLIFYING HAWAIIAN PERSPECTIVES

Kamehameha Publishing supports Kamehameha Schools' mission by publishing and distributing Hawaiian language, culture, and community-based materials that engage, reinforce, and invigorate Hawaiian cultural vitality.

Our efforts are aligned with Kamehameha Schools' Strategic Plan 2000–2015. Kamehameha Publishing also advances the Education Strategic Plan approved in 2005, which seeks to create long-term intergenerational change. Kamehameha Publishing's materials address the needs of children, parents/caregivers, educators, and communities—the four core groups identified by the Education Strategic Plan.

Kamehameha Schools was founded in 1887 by the Last Will and Testament of Princess Bernice Pauahi Bishop, the great-granddaughter of Kamehameha I. At the time of Pauahi's death, the Hawaiian population had plummeted catastrophically due to diseases introduced by foreign contact. A century after Captain James Cook arrived in Hawai'i in 1778, the Hawaiian population had dwindled from an estimated 800,000 to 47,000.

At a time of great change, Princess Pauahi anticipated that education would strengthen and sustain her people. She left nearly her entire estate—375,000 acres of land—for the foundation and perpetual operation of the Kamehameha Schools for Boys and Girls. Today, roughly 700 students a year graduate from Kamehameha Schools' three K–12 campuses on O'ahu, Maui, and Hawai'i. Kamehameha Schools operates preschools, provides preschool and postgraduate scholarships, and offers enrichment and literacy programs, giving preference to students of Hawaiian ancestry. It also provides funding for Hawaiian-focused and conversion public charter schools in predominantly Hawaiian communities.

KAMEHAMEHA SCHOOLS

▼▲▼▲▼▲▼▲▼▲▼▲▼▲▼▲▼▲▼▲▼▲▼▲▼▲▼▲▼▲▼▲▼

FIVE TIPS
FOR APPLYING THE LESSONS OF THIS BOOK

1. **ʻŌpio** (children and youth)
   In this story, the first time Kamehameha makes poi, it is lumpy. Why is the poi lumpy? Ask your mākua (parents) and kūpuna (grandparents) to teach you how to prepare your favorite foods. If the food doesn't taste right the first time, try again until it's just the way you like it.

2. **ʻOhana** (extended family)
   Remind your keiki that when Kamehameha was young, he played with his friends just like other children. But Naeʻole also makes Kamehameha work at a young age. Discuss the scene from page 8 where Kamehameha wonders why he has to plant things while his friends are out playing. Create fun activities and household routines that teach your child the value of working first and playing later.

3. **Papa kula** (classroom)
   As Kamehameha's kahu (teacher, caregiver), Naeʻole's character offers many ideas for educators. Consider the following questions and how they might apply to papa kula settings:
   • How did Naeʻole blend instruction with hands-on learning?
   • What methods did Naeʻole use to inspire the young Kamehameha and to connect his present learning with his future destiny?
   • What is the symbolism of Naeʻole's taking Kamehameha high into the ʻōhiʻa forest?
   • How did Naeʻole know when Kamehameha was ready for a new lesson? Initiate classroom activities that facilitate one-on-one interaction between teacher and student.

4. **Kaiaulu** (community)
   In the story, Naeʻole introduces Kamehameha to traditional practices—such as chanting, praying, and sharing food with others—so that "in his kulāiwi, the land of his ancestors, Kamehameha grew and thrived in his first years." How can our communities strengthen traditional practices that continue to shape the rising generations?

5. **Lāhui** (people, nation)
   Naeʻole tells Kamehameha, "We are aliʻi because of the aloha of our people." What is Naeʻole's message, and what implications does this have for communities and leaders today?

FIND OUT MORE ...

How does Kamehameha overcome challenges and fulfill his chiefly destiny?

What trials and dangers await him?

What forces propel Kamehameha to become Kanaʻiaupuni, the Conqueror of the Islands?

Read additional books in the **Kanaʻiaupuni Series** to find out!